No Dogs Allowed

by Suzanne Hardin

illustrations by Joanne Friar

Richard C. Owen Publishers, Inc.
Katonah, New York

Max and Toby saw a new sign on the beach.

It said,

"NO DOGS ALLOWED."

But dogs can't read.

So Max and Toby played on the beach.

4

They jumped in the water.

They chased the seagulls.

They dug in the sand.

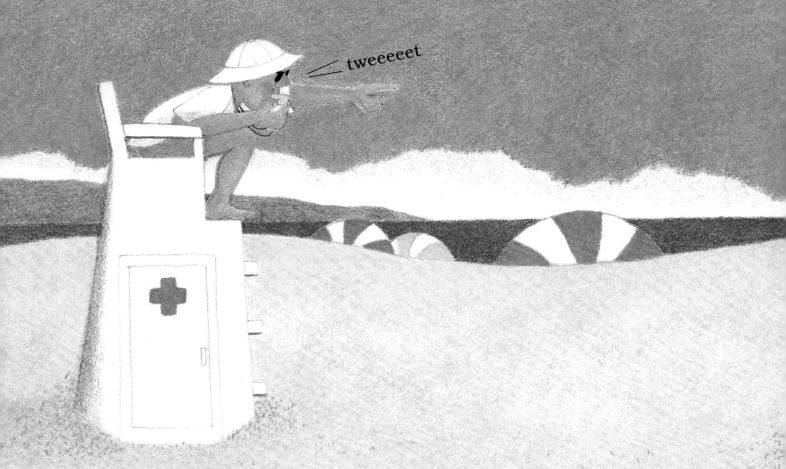

The lifeguard blew his whistle. "Tweeeeet!"

He pointed to the sign, "NO DOGS ALLOWED."

Max and Toby ran off the beach.

Dogs can't read but . . .

they had heard the ice cream truck!

ICE CREAM

jingle

jingle

jingle

-YUM